A Christmas Prayer

BY RIAN B. ANDERSON

Covenant Communications, Inc.

This book is dedicated to
Nick, Autumn, Adrian, Janille, Natalie and Tonya.

Published by Covenant Communications, Inc.
American Fork, Utah

Cover image "Four Horse Power" © Robert Duncan

Printed in Canada
First Printing: October 2001

08 07   10 9 8 7

ISBN 10: 1-57734-900-8
ISBN 13: 978-1-57734-900-6

Library of Congress Cataloging-in-Publication Data

Anderson, Rian B.
  A Christmas prayer/Rian B. Anderson
    p. cm.
  Summary: On Christmas Eve in 1881, fifteen-year-old Matt discovers the joy of giving when his father uses money intended for buying him a rifle to help a needy widow.
  ISBN 1-57734-900-8
  [1. Christmas--fiction. 2. Generosity--Fiction. 3. Frontier and pioneer life--Fiction.] I. Title.
PZ7.A54895 Ch 2001
[Fic]--dc21
                    2001042118

A Christmas Prayer

Pa never had much compassion for the lazy, or those who squandered their means and then never had enough for the necessities. But for those who were genuinely in need, his heart was as big as all outdoors. It was from him that I learned that the greatest joy in life comes from giving, not from receiving.

It was Christmas Eve, 1881. I was fifteen years old and feeling like the world had caved in on me because there just wasn't enough money to buy me the rifle that I'd wanted so bad for Christmas that year.

We did the chores early that night for some reason. I just figured Pa wanted a little extra time so we could read from the Bible. So after supper was over, I took my boots off and stretched out in front of the fireplace and waited for Pa to get down the old Bible. I was still feeling sorry for myself and, to be honest, I wasn't in much of a mood to read scriptures. But Pa didn't get the Bible; instead he bundled up and went outside. I couldn't figure it out because we had already done all the chores. I didn't worry about it long though—I was too busy wallowing in self-pity.

Soon Pa came back in. It was a cold, clear night, and there was ice in his beard. "Come on, Matt," he said. "Bundle up good; it's cold out tonight."

I was really upset then. Not only wasn't I getting the rifle for Christmas, now Pa was dragging me out in the cold, and for no earthly reason that I could see. We'd already done all the chores, and I couldn't think of anything else that needed doing, especially not on a night like this. But I knew Pa wasn't very patient with anyone who dragged their feet when he told them to do something, so I got up and put my boots back on and got my cap, coat, and mittens. Ma gave me a mysterious smile as I opened the door to leave the house. Something was up, but I didn't know what.

Outside, I became even more dismayed. There in front of the house was the work team, already hitched to the big sled. Whatever it was we were going to do wasn't going to be a short, quick, little job. I could tell. We never hitched up the big sled unless we were going to haul a big load. Pa was already up on the seat, reins in hand. I reluctantly climbed up beside him. The cold was already biting at me. I wasn't happy.

Once I was on the seat beside Pa, he pulled the sled around the house and stopped in front of the woodshed. He got off and I followed. "I think we'll put on the high sideboards," he said. "Here, help me."

The high sideboards! Whatever job we were going to do, it was a lot bigger one than I wanted to do with just the *low* sideboards on. But it would be an ever *bigger* job with the high sideboards.

When we had exchanged the sideboards, Pa went into the woodshed and came out with an armload of wood—the wood I'd spent all summer hauling down from the mountain, and then all fall sawing into blocks and splitting. What on earth was he doing? Finally I said something. "Pa," I asked, "what are you doing?"

"You been by the Widow Jensen's lately?" he asked.

The Widow Jensen lived about two miles down the road. Her husband had died a year or so before and left her with three children, the oldest being eight. Sure I'd been by, but so what? "Yeah," I said, "why?"

"I rode by just today," Pa said. "Little Jakey was out digging around in the woodpile trying to find a few chips. They're out of wood, Matt." That was all he said, and then he turned and went back into the woodshed for another armload of wood. I followed him.

We loaded the sled so high that I began to wonder if the horses would be able to pull it.

Finally, Pa called a halt to our loading. Then we went to the smokehouse and Pa took down a big ham and a side of bacon. He handed them to me and told me to put them in the sled and wait. When he returned he was carrying a sack of flour over his right shoulder, and a smaller sack of something in his left hand. "What's in the little sack?" I asked.

"Shoes. They're out of shoes. Little Jakey just had gunnysacks wrapped around his feet when he was out in the woodpile this morning. I got the children a little candy too. It just wouldn't be Christmas without a little candy."

We rode the two miles to Widow Jensen's pretty much in silence. I tried to think through what Pa was doing. We didn't have much by worldly standards. Of course, we did have a big woodpile, though most of what was left now was still in the form of logs that I would have to saw into blocks and split before we could use them. We also had meat and flour, so we could spare that, but I knew we didn't have any money, so why was Pa buying them shoes and candy? Really, why was he doing any of this? Widow Jensen had closer neighbors than us. It shouldn't have been our concern.

We came in from the blind side of the Jensen house and unloaded the wood as quietly as possible, then we took the meat and flour and shoes to the door. We knocked. The door opened a crack and a timid voice asked, "Who is it?"

"Lucas Miles, ma'am, and my son, Matt. Could we come in for a bit?"

Widow Jensen opened the door and let us in. She had a blanket wrapped around her shoulders. The children were bundled in another blanket and were sitting in front of the fireplace by a very small fire that gave off hardly any heat. Widow Jensen fumbled with a match and finally lit the lamp.

"We brought you a few things, ma'am," Pa said, and set down the sack of flour. I put the meat on the table. Then Pa handed her the sack that had the shoes in it. She opened it hesitantly and took the shoes out, one pair at a time. There was a pair for her and one for each of the children—sturdy shoes, the best—shoes that would last. I watched her carefully. She bit her lower lip to keep it from trembling, and then tears filled her eyes and started running down her cheeks. She looked up at Pa like she wanted to say something, but it wouldn't come out.

"We brought a load of wood too, ma'am," Pa said. Then he turned to me. "Matt, go bring enough in to last for awhile. Let's get that fire up to size and heat this place up."

I didn't feel like the same person when I went back out to bring in the wood. I had a big lump in my throat and, much as I hate to admit it, there were tears in my eyes too. In my mind I kept seeing those three kids huddled around the fireplace, and their mother standing there with tears running down her cheeks and so much gratitude in her heart that she couldn't speak. My heart swelled within me and a joy filled my soul that I'd

never known before. I had given presents at
Christmas many times before, but never when it
had made so much difference. I could see we were
literally saving these people's lives.

I soon had the fire blazing, and everyone's
spirits soared. The kids started giggling when Pa
handed them each a piece of candy, and Widow
Jensen looked on with a smile that probably
hadn't crossed her face for a long time. She finally
turned to us. "God bless you," she said. "I know
the Lord himself has sent you. The children and I
have been praying that He would send one of His
angels to spare us."

In spite of myself, the lump returned to my
throat and the tears welled up in my eyes again.
I'd never thought of Pa in those exact terms
before, but after Widow Jensen mentioned it I
could see that it was probably true. Suddenly I
was sure that a better man than Pa had never
walked the earth. I started remembering all the
times he had gone out of his way for Ma and me,
and for many others. The list seemed endless as I
thought on it.

Pa insisted that everyone try on the shoes
before we left. I was amazed when they all fit,
and I wondered how he had known what sizes to
get. Then I guessed that if he was on an errand
for the Lord, the Lord would make sure he got
the right sizes.

Tears were running down Widow Jensen's face
again when we stood up to leave. Pa took each of
the kids in his big arms and gave them a

hug. They clung to him and didn't want us to go. I could see that they missed their pa, and I was glad that I still had mine.

At the door, Pa turned to Widow Jensen and said, "The Missus wanted me to invite you and the children over for Christmas dinner tomorrow. The turkey will be more than the three of us can eat, and a man can get cantankerous if he has to eat turkey for too many meals. We'll be by to get you about eleven. It'll be nice to have some little ones around again. Matt here hasn't been little for quite a spell." I was the youngest. My two older brothers and two older sisters were all married and moved away.

Widow Jensen nodded and said, "Thank you, Brother Miles. I don't have to say, 'May the Lord bless you'; I know for certain that He will."

Out on the sled I felt a warmth that came from deep within, and I didn't even notice the cold. When we had gone a ways, Pa turned to me and said, "Matt, I want you to know something. Your ma and me have been tucking a little money away here and there all year so we could buy that rifle for you, but we didn't have quite enough. Then yesterday a man who owed me a little money from years back came by to make things square. Your ma and me were real excited, thinking that now we could get you that rifle, and I started in to town this morning to do just that. But on the way I saw little Jakey out scratching in the woodpile. His feet were wrapped in those gunnysacks, and I knew what I had to do.

So, son, I spent the money for shoes and a little candy for those children. I hope you understand."

I understood, and my eyes became wet with tears again. I understood very well, and I was so glad Pa had done it. Just then that rifle seemed very low on my list of priorities. Pa had given me an even better present. He had given me the look on Widow Jensen's face, and the radiant smiles of her three children.

For the rest of my life, whenever I saw any of the Jensens, or split a block of wood, I remembered—and remembering brought back that same joy I had felt riding home beside Pa that night. Pa had given me much more than a rifle that night. He had given me the best Christmas of my life.

AUTHOR'S NOTE

From a very early age, I have spent my summers high in the Manti-LaSal mountains, and my winters on Utah's west desert, herding sheep. I've learned firsthand what it means to live close to the land, and what it takes to survive in an often harsh environment. I've been a protector of the flock since before my twelfth birthday, and learned to use my own rifle even before that age.

I wrote this story while I was alone on the desert herding the sheep one winter. This is not a southern desert where the temperatures are mild. This is a more northern desert, and it is cold in the winter, traditionally dropping to twenty degrees below zero Fahrenheit around Christmas time. And it does snow; six to eight inches is common during the winter months, and I've seen storms that have brought two feet or more, accompanied by winds that blow it into five-to-seven-foot drifts.

As a sheepherder, I live in a "sheep camp"; it is a trailer, roughly seven by fourteen feet. Heat for warmth and cooking is generated by a small wood-burning stove. At night you let the fire go out so it's a more comfortable sleeping temperature. In the morning you jump out of bed, quickly start a fire in the stove, then jump back into bed until the camp warms up. When you get up in the morning, after one of those twenty-degrees-below-zero nights, there is a thick layer of frost on the inside of the windows where the moisture from your breath has frozen. There is one inch of solid ice on top of the water in the water can, and your oranges, grapefruit, eggs, and potatoes are frozen solid.

This is the kind of night I was experiencing as I wrote this story. This is why there was ice in Lucas's beard when he came back in from hitching up the team. This is why Matt didn't want to leave the warmth of the fireplace and go back out into the cold. This is why shoes and a load of wood were so critical for the Widow Jensen.

I put this type of night into a frontier setting, when a rifle was something every young man prized, and eventually needed. Matt was approaching that point in his life when he both wanted and needed his own gun.

And so you have the conflict—on the one hand, satisfying your own needs; and on the other, the critical needs of someone else. You can fulfill one or the other, but not both. Which do you choose?

All of this, and probably much, much more, funneled down and focused together in my heart that cold, clear evening as I sat alone in a sheep camp two hundred miles from home. It was a week or so before Christmas and I was thinking of what I could give my children that would have lasting value—something more than just a meaningless toy that might be forgotten five minutes after it was unwrapped. As I considered on how Christmas had become such a worldly, materialistic holiday, I pondered how I could express the true meaning of the day to my children without being preachy. This story was the result.